NIGHT BEFORE NEW YEAR'S

BY

ANNABELLE WINTERS

Copyright Notice

Books by Annabelle Winters

The CURVES FOR SHEIKHS Series

Curves for the Sheikh
Flames for the Sheikh
Hostage for the Sheikh
Single for the Sheikh
Stockings for the Sheikh
Untouched for the Sheikh
Surrogate for the Sheikh
Stars for the Sheikh
Shelter for the Sheikh
Shared for the Sheikh
Assassin for the Sheikh
Privilege for the Sheikh
Ransomed for the Sheikh
Uncorked for the Sheikh
Haunted for the Sheikh
Grateful for the Sheikh
Mistletoe for the Sheikh
Fake for the Sheikh

The CURVES FOR SHIFTERS Series

Curves for the Dragon
Born for the Bear
Witch for the Wolf
Tamed for the Lion
Taken for the Tiger

The CURVY FOR HIM Series

The Teacher and the Trainer
The Librarian and the Cop
The Lawyer and the Cowboy
The Princess and the Pirate

The CEO and the Soldier
The Astronaut and the Alien
The Botanist and the Biker
The Psychic and the Senator

THE CURVY FOR THE HOLIDAYS SERIES

Taken on Thanksgiving
Captive for Christmas
Night Before New Year's

THE CURVY FOR KEEPS SERIES

Bargain for the Boss
Given to the Groom

WWW.ANNABELLEWINTERS.COM

Night Before New Year's

BY

Annabelle Winters

1

CORRINA

"**Y**es, I'll come in to work. Of course I'll come in. No, I didn't have plans. Not really. No. No plans at all."

I hang up and stare at my phone. Five years at the hospital and I've never missed a shift, never called in sick, never even been late. Not that I've never wanted-ed to miss a shift. Not that I've never been sick. Not that I've never compromised on sleep habits, eating habits, dating habits, and pretty much *life* habits just to drag my big butt into the ER to stitch up someone who's bleeding out all over the damned tiles. They're asking more and more from us nurses, and you know what: We're damned well delivering.

So I sigh and look over at the black dress I'd put out for this New Year's Eve. Not quite a "little" black dress—that doesn't work so well when you're not that "little." But I *was* looking forward to wearing it. For some reason it hugged my hips just right, propped up my boobs perfectly, pulled in my waist, was nice and tight around my ass, like a dark, mysterious stranger's big rough hands gripping my rump firmly as he kissed me hard on the mouth and growled, "Happy New Year, baby," in a voice that sounded like a mix between Elvis and a Marvel Supervillain.

I force myself to laugh as I reach for the dress and shake my head. "Duty calls," I say with a shrug. "Duty over booty," I add with a giggle, shaking my head again as I think about the New Year's Eve party I was supposed to go to with some of my girlfriends. I wonder if my future husband is gonna be at that party, looking around for me even though he hasn't met me yet. I wonder if I'm making the wrong decision here, if maybe this once I need to choose myself over my job. I could still call the hospital back and say no. It's double overtime, with a holiday premium, of course. But though I can always use the money, it's not about the money. Truth is, they wouldn't have called me in if they weren't desperate. New Year's Eve is a drunken, wild night in this city. People do stupid, reckless things, and half the time those stupid, reckless things land them in my ER, gasping and groaning, screaming and howling, bleeding and sometimes dying.

"Not if I can help it," I say softly to that silent black dress that's shining in the yellow light of my bedroom. "Nobody dies on Nurse Coco's shift. They need me at the hospital tonight. Future husband can wait. He'll wait, right?"

I stand there like an idiot, wondering if I'm seriously talking to an inanimate object. I force out a laugh and reach for the dress again, but as I turn to the closet, it feels like the dress is talking back.

"Wear me anyway," the dress whispers. "Go on. Wear me anyway."

I raise an eyebrow and wonder if I put any whiskey in my coffee this morning. Eyebrow still raised, I look the dress up and down, thinking about how it hugged my curves so well, made me feel confident and sexy. The scrubs we wear are baggy, shapeless, and loose. I could hike the dress up over my butt and put my scrubs on over it, couldn't I? It's tight enough to stay in place. And it'll be my secret. My dirty little secret.

I lean my head back and laugh at how tame and innocent my "dirty little secret" actually is. It would be different if I wore super-hot black lingerie under my scrubs. Whatever. I am who I am.

"All right, talking dress," I say. "You're on. It's kind of a party in the ER on New Year's Eve, isn't it? And maybe future husband will roll in with a hamster up his butt or something, saying he has no idea how it got there."

And now I'm laughing, and I'm dressing, and before I know it I'm on my way, little black dress hiked up over my bum in secret, a strange feeling of anticipation rolling through me as I drive towards the setting sun.

"Happy New Year, baby," I growl in my Supervillain Elvis voice, cracking myself up but also sending a ripple of excitement through me as I wonder if maybe I just made the *right* choice, if future husband is gonna show up at *this* party and not the other one. "Happy New Year."

2

CAIN

"**T**here's nothing happy about it," I growl to the grinning intern in scrubs who's clearly delirious because he probably hasn't slept in three fucking days. I remember being a med-school intern, full of hope and ambition, ready to save the world. And then you grow up and see that people don't want to be saved, that the world is beyond saving, that hope is a fucking illusion, like unicorns and fairies.

"What's with the asshole new doctor?" I hear the intern say way too loudly, the caffeine and uppers clearly messing with his judgment.

Though maybe the little shit's judgment isn't that far off, I think grimly as I stop in my tracks and clench my massive fists that want to make contact with the intern's jaw, maybe knock out a couple of his caffeine-stained teeth. See how happy he is when he whistles every time he talks.

Yeah, maybe he's not so far off, I think again as I force my temper back to its hiding place in my dark, tormented soul. I *am* a fucking asshole.

And so I grin and shrug, shake my head and continue my rounds of the scene in the ER. The sun has just set, and it's relatively calm in here. The calm before the storm that's New Year's Eve.

The wail of an ambulance makes me wince, and I rub my temples as I remind myself of the doctor's oath I took years ago, the oath I'm supposed to renew every year:

Do no harm.

That's the first responsibility of a medical professional. It's beautifully simple in a way, isn't it? Forget trying to cure every disease, heal every wound, fix everything that's broken. Start with the fucking basics: Do no harm. Don't make things worse than they are. That's the starting point. The goddamn beginning.

Except this isn't the beginning, I think as I let that old anger ooze through my hard, chiseled frame like a drug. Anger that's been festering in me for ten long years, ever since I lost my little girl in a room just like this, on a night just like this.

"Nah, this isn't the beginning," I whisper to myself as I glance at the ticking clock and remind myself of what I came here to do, why I'm here in this city, in this hospital. "It's the end. It ends here. It ends tonight. I'm gonna finish it, and then I'm gonna find peace at last. Peace forever."

"Peace out, kid," comes a woman's voice from my left, and I whip my head around like I've been punched in the face. Yeah, the ER isn't chaos yet, but it's never a quiet place, even at the slowest times. There's beeping and buzzing of a hundred machines, screeching of wheelchairs and gurneys, the voices of doctors and nurses, interns and receptionists, patients insisting that their stubbed toe is more important than the groaning dude with a kitchen-knife sticking out of his arm.

But for some reason this woman's voice cuts

through the background noise like that kitchen-knife slicing through butter, and when I turn to look at her I almost fall to my knees, almost reach out for fucking life support, a shot to revive my heart that I swear stopped for a moment that lasted eternity.

"Holy Mother of God," I groan as I feel my loose scrubs tighten as my cock fills out so fast I get dizzy from the blood leaving my buzzing head. "What the fuck just happened?"

It's been years since I even gave a woman a second look, let alone reacted like this. And no doubt I'm fucking *reacting*. I'm full hard, nothing but my tight underwear holding my cock back from tenting my scrubs in a way that would make the entire ER go into cardiac arrest. She's one of the ER nurses, and I'm staring like a wretched barbarian at her magnificent ass as she leans in to touch the forehead of a teenage girl with heavy black eyeshadow and an expression that clearly says, "I took some pills and now I'm scared I'm gonna die!"

"Peace out, kid," the nurse says to the teen again, her pretty face lit up in a smile that I swear lights a candle in my dark heart even as it lights a fire in my thick cock. "You're going to be just fine. The effects will wear out in a few hours, and you'll be able to bring in the new year with your friends, OK? Just stay out of your parents' medicine cabinet from now on, yeah?"

The drugged-up kid turns bright red and nods sheepishly, relief washing over her as this nurse's compassion and confidence flows through the air in a way I swear I can almost smell. I take a deep breath and nod. Fuck, I *can* smell her, can't I? Natural body spray, I can tell.

And a natural body, I think as I shamelessly admire her strong hourglass shape, take in the sight of her wide, womanly hips, imagine myself holding on to that big bottom as I plunge my throbbing cock into her. I lick my lips as I wonder what her nipples look like beneath those scrubs. Big like dinner-plates, I decide. And that's what I want for dinner.

I almost laugh out loud at how quickly my thoughts are going to places they haven't been in years. Maybe going to places they've never been at all. This is all new, isn't it? All new. Like a new beginning. A new—

"You must be the new doctor!" comes her voice through my churning mind. "Hi! I'm Corrina." She looks down at her nametag, which is perched right where I want my mouth to be—on the apex of her glorious left breast. "But everyone calls me Coco. Come to think of it, I need to get a new nametag." She glances at my white coat and raises an eyebrow. "And you need a new nametag too. How will everyone get to know you if they don't know your name?"

"What difference does it make? I'm not going to be here long," I say, my head still buzzing as I lock eyes with Coco and feel something shift inside me—and not just my goddamn cock. It's a cosmic shift, earth-shattering and groundbreaking, like suddenly everything's changed, like the entire reason I got

myself transferred to this hospital maybe isn't what
I thought it was, like maybe unicorns really do exist,
that maybe there is such a thing as hope, as fate, as
destiny.

Maybe there is such a thing as love.

"Why aren't you going to be here long?" Coco says
with a quizzical frown. "They told me you just transferred here. You going somewhere, Doctor . . . ?"

"Cain," I say like I'm in a stupor. "My name's Cain."

She blinks as the name registers, and I wonder if
she's read the Old Testament. Cain, son of Adam, the
bad kid who murdered his own brother. Of course, I
never had a brother, and my own parents weren't re-
ligious or anything. Hell, they could barely even read.
Don't know why they named me that. Don't know
why I kept the name. Clearly this woman didn't seem
locked into the name she'd been given.

"What's wrong with Corrina?" I say. "I like Corrina.
I'm going to call you Corrina."

"Then I'm going to call you what the rest of the
staff is calling you," she mutters, her jaw tightening
as she stares up at me defiantly.

"You mean asshole?" I say with a grin. Fuck, this
woman has fire in her, doesn't she. Doesn't like someone trying to exercise control over her. And that
makes me want to exercise control over her. Own
her. Possess her. Fucking *take* her.

"*Doctor* Asshole, actually," she says, immediate-
ly covering her mouth and gasping. "Ohmygod,
I *so* didn't mean to say that! Nobody calls you that!
I swear it!"

"Oh, really?" I say in a slow drawl as my head buzzes
with an excitement I haven't felt since I was a teen-

ager chasing everything in a skirt and heels. I step close to her, my body shuddering as I have to fight my need to touch her, to pull her into me, to kiss those red lips, smell her lustrous hair, taste her sweetness. "So if nobody calls me that, doesn't it mean you just came up with the name Doctor Asshole?"

"Oh, fuck, I'm gonna get fired today, aren't I?" she groans, rubbing her eyes and shaking her head. "I mean, oh *shucks*. Oops. OK, I'm gonna stop talking now. Hi! I'm Coco! What's your name? Ohmygod, am I still talking?!"

I love you, I think as I stare in amused disbelief at this curvy, vivacious nurse who's somehow both flustered and confident at the same time, like she doesn't have any filters, is just . . . just *herself*.

"You can't help it, can you?" I say, her sweetness and exuberance getting to me finally as I break into a smile—a smile that feels real, a smile that feels honest, a smile that feels like there's still hope, like maybe tonight isn't going to be the end after all, like maybe . . . just maybe . . .

"Help what?" she says, pulling my mind away from that dark hole where it's lived for a decade, consumed by grief and hatred, the need for revenge, for justice.

"Help being yourself," I say softly, stepping close enough that we're almost touching.

"Who else would I be?" she says, blinking and looking away like she's embarrassed at the compliment.

Mine, comes the thought as I look into her big brown eyes, feel the world melt away like I'm being drawn into her world. *That's who you're going to be before the end of the night.*

She blinks again and lets out a soft gasp, and I

wonder if I just said that out loud. No, I didn't. But I swear it feels like somehow she got the message, that she feels what I'm feeling too, that she understands that before the night is done, she's going to be mine.

Mine for just one night, though, I think as I remember why I'm here, what I came here to do, what I've waited patiently for ten years to do.

Just one night.

3
COCO

"**J**ust one night," I say to the younger nurses, smiling as I wipe my brow with a square of sterile gauze and then change my gloves for like the hundredth time tonight. It's only eight, but shit's already getting crazy, and I wonder if it's also a full moon or something. My coworkers are stressed and harried, shaking their heads and muttering under their breath every time the front doors slide open and another New Year's Eve casualty stumbles in bleeding because they got drunk too early, choking because they popped too many pills, limping because they didn't see the curb or the stairs. There's even some dude with a dogbite on his arm. Maybe even the animals are going crazy.

But although the chaos is building around me, inside I feel calm and steady. My body is humming with energy, buzzing with excitement, thrumming with what feels like music. I've never felt like this before, and I try to push away the thought that the feeling took over after that brief moment of closeness with that new doctor: That tall, brooding, darkly handsome doctor whose green eyes did something to me.

"What was Doctor Asshole saying to you earlier?" says the receptionist as I stop by her desk to steal a piece of candy from the dish she hides behind the counter.

"Just that he knows we're already calling him Doctor Asshole," I say with a wink, barely chewing the bite-sized Snickers before grabbing another.

"Ohmygod, no!" she says, covering her mouth. "He didn't hear me say that, did he?"

"Nope," I say, slipping one more treat into my pocket and turning back to the battlefield that's my job. "He heard *me* say it."

I'm back in the fray before I hear her reply, and I glance across the room and see Doctor Cain working on a meth-head who's got a piece of stained glass sticking out of his thigh. What the hell did he do? Jump through a church window?

I snicker at the thought, and then I steal a moment to take in the sight of Doctor Cain at work. Soon a shudder goes through my body when I realize that shit, this guy is good. Surly and brooding, yeah. Not a great bedside manner, no. But he's still damned good in the ER, where speed is everything, where taking an extra minute to ask someone how their evening is going might mean someone else bleeds out behind the next curtain.

"OK, stop it," I mutter when I realize I'm staring at the tall, muscular Doctor Cain. But I can't look away, and I absentmindedly pop the last piece of candy into my mouth and keep staring like an idiot.

He's older, ruggedly handsome, with streaks of gray in his hair and stubble, lines creasing his forehead and face. He's been through chaos and madness before, I can tell. He's been through more than that, maybe. It's hardened him.

His body is hard too, I notice. Broad and muscled like a beast, with massive shoulders and a heavy chest. And those forearms! They're thick like trees, veins popping out in high relief as he deftly slides the glass shard out from the patient's thigh and cleans the wound vigorously as the meth addict howls like a beaten dog.

"The pain means you haven't got nerve damage," I hear Cain saying to the thrashing man, and I watch in fascination as the massive doctor holds the addict down with one arm and then . . . then . . . then looks over at me.

"Come here," he commands, beckoning with his head in a supremely arrogant way that should piss me off but instead makes my buttocks tighten and my nipples firm up. He's looking right into my eyes, his gaze unwavering, his hard body unmoving even as his patient moans and writhes under his grasp.

I blink and look to my left like I'm wondering if he's talking to someone else. But I know he's talking to me, and I briskly walk over, trying to look as professional as I can even though I think I have bits of chocolate all over my mouth.

"Hold on," I say, looking over at the nurse's station for a new face-mask. "I need to—"

"Don't worry about it," Doctor Cain says. "It's safe enough so long as you don't drool all over your patient. Those masks don't do shit anyway. If anything, they're receptacles for germs, and every time you breathe through that shit you're spraying a fucking jetstream of microbes all over your doomed patient. Besides, I want to talk to you, and I need to see your lips."

The meth-head squeals with panicked laughter, and half the ER looks over at Doctor Cain and then at me like they sense the energy between us, feel the crackle of electricity in the air, see the spark that I feel in my core and somehow know he feels in his.

"Um, all right," I say, walking over to Cain as I try to ignore my coworkers' raised eyebrows. "What would you like me to do?"

"Stitch this fucker up while I hold him down," Cain says matter-of-factly, and I frown at his language even though it makes me want to smile. The ER can get slap-happy at times, and after you've been working in the madness for a while you get a bit loose with the language. Still, there's probably a line Doctor Cain is crossing here. It's almost like he doesn't give a shit about his job, about what people say about him, about anything really.

But when I get close and see the way he looks at me, I feel like maybe I'm wrong. Maybe he *does* give a damn about something.

And maybe that something is . . . is . . . me?

I push away the thought as I prepare the needle and bio-thread. I'm good at this, and soon I'm totally focused on the task, on the details, my gloved fingers deftly pushing the needle through skin quickly and cleanly, minimizing the pain even though I get the weird feeling that Doctor Cain doesn't give a damn about how much pain this poor patient feels.

"So, you come here often?" Cain whispers to me just then, and I flinch as I snort with surprised laughter. The needle jabs the meth-head, and he howls again as I realize I'm getting pulled into this crazy state of mind that's oozing from this dark, mysterious doctor, this arrogant man with an edge that's making my panties damp.

"OK, we're both gonna lose our licenses," I say through a tight smile as I glance apologetically at my patient. "This isn't the time, and it most certainly isn't the place."

"We can get outta here," says Cain matter-of-factly. He holds the meth-head down with his strong arm and casually looks at his watch. It's a Rolex, I notice. A twenty-thousand dollar watch. I glance up at the streaks of gray in Cain's thick dark hair, the lines of experience marking his forehead, that strange desolation in his deep green eyes. Who is this man, I wonder. And why does he make me feel this way? Why am I actually enjoying this? Why do I feel like this entire moment is about us, that maybe this entire night is about us?

"Shouldn't I finish sewing him up first, Doctor?" I respond.

"Meh," says Cain with a shrug and a grin. "I think we just slap some duct-tape on the last couple of inches."

"That's actually something you can do in an emergency," I say hurriedly to the wide-eyed patient while thanking the heavens that he's too jacked up to understand what's going on. Wait, do *I* understand what's going on? What the hell am I doing?! This is serious shit! I'm a nurse, a professional, a responsible, sensible woman! Why am I acting like I'm drunk?!

I glance into Cain's green eyes, and for a moment I see a spark in them. But then he blinks and that darkness returns like it's been there so long it's just

normal for him. Something in me reaches out to him
like I want to heal him, fix him, patch him up. It's
the healer in me, the driving force that makes me do
what I do, makes me work twelve-hour shifts until
my feet get corns and calluses and there are varicose
veins crisscrossing my legs like it's a freakin' map of
America's rivers.

Quickly I finish sewing up my patient, and when
I look at my handiwork I realize it's actually pretty
neat and clean. Not a loose thread. The sutures are
tight and precise.

"Don't scratch it," I say gently to the man like I'm
talking to a puppy who's just gotten back from the
vet. Immediately the meth-head begins to scratch,
and I slap his hand away sternly. "What did I just tell
you? Don't scratch! No! Stop!"

"Yes, Ma'am," says the guy, his bugged-out eyes
looking like they're gonna pop out and bounce away
into the night. He glances at Cain and back at me,
nodding again submissively like he's just been scold-
ed by Mommy and Daddy.

I fold my arms beneath my boobs as the patched-
up patient slides off the table with a grateful smile. I
know that everyone is still staring at me like I've lost
it, but I don't care. I glance over at Cain, who's standing right next to me, his thick arms folded across his
broad, heavy chest. For a moment I get the surreal
sense that Cain and I really are proud parents, and I
have to blink away the feeling that I'm being pulled
into some alternate reality.

"I think there was something in that candy bar,"
I mutter as *this* reality finally sinks in and I feel my

face go flush when I think of my totally unprofessional behavior. "I've heard of people injecting drugs through the wrapper."

"Candy is already packed with the worst fucking drug on the market," says Cain, glancing at his watch again. "It's called sugar."

"Well then, I'm a hardcore addict," I say with a laugh, shaking my head and strolling to the wash station to clean up and get ready for whatever comes next.

"We all have our vices," says Cain, walking right alongside me like we're in the freakin' park or something. "If sugar is your worst one, then you're probably as innocent as I thought."

I raise an eyebrow at him as I feel a tingle between my legs. I think of the black dress I've got on beneath my shapeless scrubs. A dress that's hiked up over my hips. Suddenly an image of myself with my palms flat against the cool blue walls of the hospital injects itself into my head. I gasp as I see myself clear as day, vivid as night, that black dress hiked all the way up past my boobs, Doctor Cain taking me from behind as the entire ER staff hoot and holler, everyone counting down to the New Year like they're all part of this weirdness that's unfolding like a sick, surreal play.

"Nobody's innocent," I say, not sure why we're talking in cryptic innuendos but feeling like it's somehow apt.

"Original sin?" he says. "Ah, so you *have* read the Old Testament."

I hesitate a moment. Then I nod. "I know the story of Cain, if that's what you mean."

He looks at his watch for the third time.

"OK, if you're trying to show off your fancy watch, I already noticed," I say with a smirk. "Thanks for reminding me of the economic disparity between doctors and nurses."

"My, my," he drawls. "Such big words. They teach you kids about that in nursing school?"

"You know, you really *are* an asshole," I snap, shaking my head and raising my eyebrows. "Get out of my way. I've got patients to see."

But Cain doesn't budge from my path, and I gasp when I see that he's got me boxed in against the washing station in the corner of the bustling ER. Only now do I notice how big he really is, how broad his shoulders are, how thick his upper arms are beneath his scrubs. Again I feel a tingle between my legs as I fight the image of Cain taking me right here, on New Year's Eve, emptying himself into me with wild desperation, filling me like it's the last night before the end of the world or something.

"So do I," he whispers. "I've got patients to see too, Nurse Coco. One patient in particular. He's in the East Wing lockdown. And you're going to take me there."

I feel the walls closing in as I look up into Cain's eyes and see no sign of that spark, like maybe it was never there, like maybe what I thought was a moment was just manipulation, a mind-trick, a mistake.

"What the hell are you talking about?" I say. "The East Wing is closed for renovation. It has been for almost a year now. There's no one there. Not even the construction guys. They have the night off. What are you—"

"Shut up and do what I say," Cain growls, grabbing my wrists and quickly glancing over to see if anyone's looking. "Do what I say, and maybe I'll let you live."

4

CAIN

I almost laugh at how convincing I sound. Like a psycho-killer or some shit. I'm certainly not going to kill this sweetheart of a nurse. Yeah, I want to hold her down, spank that big, round ass, fuck her so hard all the ECGs in the building go haywire. But the only person I'm gonna kill is the motherfucker lying in a coma in the East Wing of this hospital.

In a coma, and under the protection of the FBI.

"I've been waiting for years for Doctor Death to show up on the radar again," I say to Coco as I lead her down the stairs and along the empty passageway towards the East Wing that's supposedly closed for construction. "I thought he was going down for his crimes ten years ago, but the fucking feds cut a deal with him, gave him immunity and put him into witness protection."

"OK, you're sounding like a paranoid delusional," Coco says, her voice shaky but calm, like she's had years of experience dealing with a crisis, years of experience seizing control of herself and then the situation. "I can help, Cain. Just listen to me, all right? There is *no one* in the East Wing. It's shut down and closed off. Maybe you haven't slept well. Maybe you're taking something. Maybe you *need* to be taking something."

I need to be taking *you*, comes the thought as I look down at Coco, her pretty round face shining like the moon under the overhead lights of the long passageway. Again those feelings try to push through my resolve, and I close my eyes and clench my jaw as I fight back the desire that died when my little girl died, when I swore that I was never going to expose myself to the pain and anguish of losing a child again.

Of course, the only way to guarantee that was to never *have* another child.

And the only way to guarantee *that* was to never have a woman, never fall in love, never start a family.

I cock my head and frown as I see how crazy my logic is, how maybe I *am* off the rails, like maybe I really *should've* gone to therapy after losing little Maggie in that ER all those years ago. But I was too proud, too angry, too fucking *macho* to sit in a room and "talk about it" with some shrink back then.

I suddenly stop in the empty hallway, letting go of Coco's wrists and slamming my big palms against the pastel-blue walls.

"What the fuck am I doing?" I groan, grinning and shaking my head even though the only thing funny about this is me. "Hell, I'm sorry, OK? I don't mean to scare you. I'm not going to hurt you. Just get me into the East Wing and you can go. You can call the cops or whatever. It won't matter by then. It'll be over by then."

I take long, deep breaths as I feel Coco's calming presence by my side. Slowly I look up, realizing she's standing right beside me even though I guess she could high-tail it down the hallway, pull the fire-alarm, scream for help.

Except she won't, I understand as a dizzying warmth goes through my cold, hard body. She won't scream for help.

She *is* help.

That warmth slowly creeps through my frame like I really am on something, and I stand up straight and turn to her as my head buzzes with that excitement I felt when I first laid eyes on this vision of bubbly beauty.

"You're looking at me with pity," I say softly. "Like you feel sorry for me. You really think I'm fucking crazy, don't you?"

Coco blinks and shakes her head. "It's called compassion, Cain. You're hurting, and my whole life is about sensing hurt in others. Healing hurt in others. Making the pain go away. Talk to me, Cain. Just talk, OK?"

I blink in disbelief. I just met this woman, just shared a giddy, flirtatious moment with her in the ER, just pulled her into the hallway by force while babbling about some secret wing in the hospital like this is a fucking horror movie. And now she's standing her ground, looking at me with those big brown eyes, daring me to open up to her?! Is this real?

"OK," Coco says, her voice wavering for a moment but still she goes on just with the strength of her will. "If you won't talk, then I will. Just listen, Cain. Listen until you feel comfortable talking."

I stare in wonder as Coco leans against the wall and

takes a breath, that compassionate smile breaking wide on her round face, making her look like an angel under the overhead lights. I want to kiss her, love her, fucking *be* with her. But I can't. I need to finish what started ten years ago. Finish my dark journey and leave this lonely life, join my baby-girl in the afterlife. There's nothing for me here, is there?

Is there?

"You joked about not having a brother earlier," Coco says. "I actually did have a brother. He died when I was five. A genetic defect of some sort, they said. Complications and whatnot. I was too young to understand, and my parents were too uneducated to really explain it to me later."

I look at her and nod, pushing away that warmth and steeling my resolve yet again. This could just be her stalling for time, I tell myself. Waiting for a chance to jab me with a syringe and then run for the hills. "And that's what drove you to become a nurse? Great fucking story. I feel like I read that in *Cosmo* or something. Or maybe it was *Penthouse Letters*."

I don't know if I want to piss her off, push her away, stop her from getting under my skin. But she just laughs and rises up to my challenge, those big brown eyes narrowing just enough to reveal that this sweet little nurse is more complicated than she seems, that there's more than some simple sob-story of losing a brother and becoming a nurse behind what she's telling me.

"*Penthouse Letters*?" she says with a raised eyebrow. "Oh, so *you're* the one sending in all those stories of doctors having their way with nurses."

I grin at the way she's refusing to be deterred by me being a fucking asshole to her, and it's melting me like butter. "Wishful thinking," I whisper as my cock reminds me that even with all the drama it's been hard and ready, champing at the bit to be let loose, make this fantasy real.

"Keep wishing, Doctor," she says firmly, making me grin wider at the way she's changing the mood here, turning things around in the most beautiful way, making me think of magic and not murder, making me feel like this is a first date and not the last act of a man consumed by hate.

"Oh, I will, Nurse Coco," I say as she leans against the wall and I place my palms on either side of her head. "And tonight's the night wishes come true, don't they? New Year's Eve?"

"Yeah, that's not a thing," says Coco. "Now where were we?"

"*Penthouse Letters*," I say, shamelessly glancing at her neckline and gasping as I see a hint of cleavage, see the swell of her healthy boobs, imagine the outline of her big nipples. I claw at the wall as I force myself to hold back, remind myself of why I'm here, try to tell myself that this curvy nurse has got me turned around and could very well fuck up my plans.

"Focus, Doctor Cain," she says, looking right into my eyes like a goddamn hypnotist. I can see the strength in her eyes, hear it in her voice. She's been through something too, hasn't she, it occurs to me. Something that built up strength and compassion in her. Maybe I should fucking listen to her cheesy story of why she become a sweet, loving nurse.

"OK, you got thirty seconds," I say with a grin,

glancing at my watch and then back at her. "Thirty seconds to tell me about your heartbreaking sob story that inspired you to become a nurse. So your brother died in the hospital when you were a kid. Boo fucking hoo. What next? You saved a puppy from the animal shelter and suddenly you decided you were Mother Theresa?"

"You know, if you redirected some of the effort you put into being an asshole, you might actually be a damned good doctor," she says without missing a beat.

"I *am* an asshole. It doesn't take any effort," I shoot back.

"Character takes effort. It's all about the choices you make, the actions you take." She shrugs. "Even being an asshole takes effort, whether you admit it or not. So why not put that effort into—"

"Into what? Saving the damned world?" I can't believe I'm suddenly getting pulled into some deep-ass conversation that's making me feel things I don't want to feel.

Making me feel like a human being again.

Like a doctor again.

Like a man again.

A man who's looking into the eyes of his woman.

"Who are you?" I mutter suddenly, almost unconsciously. It's not a real question. I don't expect her to say she's an undercover cop or the real JFK assassin or Taylor Swift in disguise.

Nah, it's not a real question . . .

Because I already know the answer:

She's mine—that's who she is.

She's fucking *mine*.

"Why are you looking at me like that?" she whispers, touching her hair as her steady gaze wavers for a moment, like she feels this weird sexual tension, this sense of danger mixing with arousal, this feeling of fate, like this moment is about us and nothing else.

I close my eyes and bite my lip so hard I draw blood. Of all the hospitals in America, I end up at this one, on this night, with this nurse.

"My brother didn't die in a hospital," she says, and I blink and frown, realizing she's picking up the conversation after I rolled my eyes about her sob-story. "He died at home, before my parents understood what was happening, what needed to be done, what could have been done." She pauses and swallows. "What *should* have been done."

I blink as I finally start to focus on Coco and not myself, on what *she's* feeling and not what *I'm* feeling. The change of focus happens so quickly I don't notice until I feel tears rolling down my cheeks, tears that puzzle me. I'm not crying, am I? I can't be crying. Tough guys don't cry. Why the fuck am I crying?!

"It's called empathy," Coco says softly, blinking away her own tears with a sweet smile that lights up the blue hallways and makes it feel like morning, the morning of a new day, a new life, a new . . . year?

"Empathy," I whisper, smiling and slowly caressing her cheek with the back of her hand. "I've heard of that. I think they mentioned it in med school. What does it mean again?"

"Putting yourself in another's shoes," she whispers, turning her head slightly as I cup her face and draw closer, so close I can smell every part of her body, almost fucking taste her. "Making the effort to feel what they're feeling. It's a uniquely human ability, you know. Making yourself feel what someone else is feeling."

"And what are you feeling right now, Nurse Coco?" I whisper as the blue pastel walls swaddle us like we're newborn babes.

She giggles and shrugs. "You tell me, Doctor Cain. Empathy, remember? Put yourself in my shoes."

I take a breath and exhale slowly. Then I nod. I'll play her game. We've got all night. "Well, let's see," I say, reaching around and sliding my hand down the curve of her back but stopping just above her magnificent ass. I know once I get my hands on there I'm not stopping until the clock strikes twelve. I look deep into her eyes, reaching for that strange feeling Coco brought out in me—that ability to feel what someone else is feeling. It's the feeling that drives all of us in the medical profession, isn't it? Yeah, maybe it gets buried and diluted after years of dealing with the craziness of the hospital, but it's still there somewhere.

Somewhere.

5
COCO

I feel like I'm somewhere else. On an island maybe, surrounded by blue sky even though I know it's the pastel blue of the hospital walls. I'm topsy-turvy with the madness of just the past few . . . wait, how long has it even *been* since I started my shift? I have no damned idea! It could be twenty minutes. It could be twenty years. I've lost all sense of time and space, it feels.

"What am I feeling?" I hear myself ask Doctor Cain as I shudder in his strong arms, breathe deep of his manly scent that's overwhelming me like the musk of an alpha beast in heat. My panties are wet beneath my scrubs, and I can barely acknowledge how aroused I am, how my arousal started the moment Cain looked at me across that crowded ER, how it heightened as I sewed up that poor meth-head and cracked dark jokes that brought out the worst in me, made me remember that I always had an edge, that along with a heightened ability to feel compassion, pity, and empathy, I also had a dark side.

A dark side that drove my choices almost as much as my need to heal drove me. I'm not shaken by the sight of blood, not deterred by people screaming and crying, panicking and even dying. Yes, that side of me drove a lot of my choices.

Especially the choice to still be standing here.

"What you're *not* feeling is fear," Cain says after he looks at me with those dark green eyes like he's evaluating me. "Even though I just threatened to kill you. Am I that unconvincing as a psycho-killer?"

I laugh. "Oh, you're *very* convincing—as a psycho, at least. As for the killer part . . . well, we've all had patients die under our watch, haven't we?"

Cain snorts in surprise, grinning wide and pulling me closer. "Fuck, you're something, aren't you?" He sighs as the smile fades, and then nods like he understands that those of us who've been in the healthcare business for years have developed this hard exterior, this protective shell, this shield around our deepest emotions. In some ways the ER is a brutal, ruthless place, with split-second decisions being made with imperfect information. Decisions that are sometimes wrong. Decisions that sometimes result in death. If you crack every time you make an innocent mistake, you'll never make it to the next shift, never get the chance to save the next kid who gets rushed in with a gunshot wound.

But some wounds don't heal, do they, I think as I see the decades-old pain in Cain's eyes, study the lines on his lean handsome face that's weathered the storms of emotion that all of us in this world have had to ride out.

"What else?" I whisper, feeling this need to keep pushing, keep probing, diagnosing, searching . . . reaching. At first I thought Cain might just be unhinged, a paranoid delusional. Maybe even on something. It's shockingly common in the medical profession, when doctors have access to all kinds of mind-bending medications, are under all kinds of stress. But now I don't think it's that simple. Cain's eyes are clear and focused, and his body is lean and healthy. I can feel his hard muscle against me, and I blink and gasp when I realize that he's holding me like I'm his, holding me like no man's ever held me, holding me like he never wants to let go, holding me like this is both the first night and the last night of our time together, like the clock is ticking down to something more serious than just another New Year's Day.

"You feel . . . sorry for me," Cain whispers, his face hardening for a flash. Then he blinks and shakes his head quickly. "Nah, that's not it. It's not pity. It's . . . it's . . ." He trails off, a puzzled look in his eyes. "It's . . . love. It's love, isn't it?"

I almost choke as I see how damned serious he is. "Um, what?" I mumble. "OK, maybe you need a bit more practice in this empathy game, Doctor Cain."

"Empathy," he mutters. "Putting yourself in someone else's shoes. Feeling what they're feeling. Feeling it deeply. Feeling it like they're your own feelings."

"Well, once you feel something, it *is* your own feeling," I say, not sure what we're talking about but in a way totally sure what we're talking about. We're talking about us. Us as individuals. Us as a man and woman whose choices brought us to this point in time, where we're in each other's arms somewhere in a twilight zone with blue pastel walls, a clock ticking down to midnight.

Is this my Cinderella story, I wonder as I see my

words hit home for him in a way I don't quite understand. It's like he's opening up to something. Maybe to himself. To why he's here. What he's come here to do.

And then reality comes busting in like someone breaking down the door, and I look wildly around me as I remember that this strange new doctor dragged me out of the ER and babbled something about a secret wing in the hospital where the FBI is holding patients or something crazy like that!

"You think I'm crazy," he whispers, leaning in closer and caressing my smooth cheek in a way that should freak me out but instead makes me shudder in the most sensual way. "Unhinged. Delusional. Like I've snapped or something. And although a part of you is scared, looking for a way out, there's another part of you that wants to help me." Suddenly his eyes snap back into focus. He glances down the empty hallway and then back at me. "So help me, Nurse Coco. Help me kill the doctor who murdered my daughter."

I blink like twenty times and almost laugh out loud at how absurd this sounds. I mean, I'm a nurse, a professional, a student of medical history. I know that even smart, functional people can suffer from paranoia and delusions. But there's something about Doctor Cain that excites me more than it scares me. And yeah, although he's right in that I felt sorry for him, that's not the biggest part of what I'm feeling.

Ohmygod, this man is so confident, so serious, so sure of what he thinks is going on in this closed-down hospital wing that I'm getting pulled into it like Alice in Wonderland tumbling down the rabbit hole! I'm getting sucked into this man's story, into the darkness and danger, the excitement and sheer madness of it! It's like it doesn't even matter if we spend the evening exploring empty rooms, looking for some secret government hideout where they're conducting alien autopsies or whatever. All that matters is what we're feeling. All that matters is tonight. This one night. The night before New Year's.

"OK, just so I understand," I say softly, gasping as I realize we've moved closer to one another even though we've got all the space in the world around us. Cain isn't restraining me anymore. He's just . . . holding me. Holding me like I'm his. Holding me like I'm his story, his Happy New Year, his forever. Like I'm his, and that's what these feelings are about. All the feelings. Pity and fear. Giddiness and joy. Darkness and madness. All of it.

"Go on, Nurse Coco," he says sternly, smiling as I feel his warm breath on my lips. "I'm listening. What's your assessment of the situation?"

"Just so I understand . . ." I continue. "You believe your daughter was murdered by *another* doctor. And you've been tracking that killer doctor—"

"Doctor Death," Cain says matter-of-factly.

"Sorry, what?"

"That's what I call him. Doctor Death."

"Sure," I say, almost laughing as I wonder if we're in a cartoon now. "Let's go with that. Now, how long ago did this happen?"

"Ten years, three months, and four days. Six months after I got Maggie. Six months was all I had with her, and then she was taken from me."

I blink as I see the clarity and focus in Cain's eyes. If he's delusional, he's pretty darned convincing. I bet he'd pass a lie detector test. Maybe the FBI has one down here in their secret hideout.

"I'm so sorry, Cain," I whisper, shuddering as I feel his grief, almost crying as it occurs to me that there's no difference between *real* feelings and *imagined* feelings. They're all the same to the brain, aren't they? "To lose a six-month-old child . . . I can't even imagine how hard it must have been for you and your . . . your wife."

I frown as suddenly reality interrupts me and I realize that if there was a daughter, there must be a mother somewhere in this story too. Who is she? Where is she? More importantly, *what* is she? Real or imagined? Alive or dead? His lover or his ex?

"Maggie was nine," Cain says. Then he frowns like he senses what I'm thinking. "And there's no wife. Never was." He holds up his left hand. "See? No ring. No bling."

I glance at his ring finger, and I'm almost angry at myself for being delighted that there isn't even a tan line. Well, that's good. Story proceeding as planned. Carry on.

"Noted," I say, trying to keep a straight face. Then I try to do some math. "So Maggie was nine when she died. And you'd only had her for six months? You got custody? Or did your wife—sorry, I mean Maggie's mother—um . . . did she . . . did something happen?"

Ohmygod, am I now hoping Cain's dead daughter's mother is dead too? What's *wrong* with me?!

"She passed away," Cain says with a shrug like he barely knew her. "She was a widow. No next of kin, so I legally adopted Maggie."

I blink and then blink again. "Adoption? Your daughter was adopted?" I think a moment and then frown. Never married. Barely knew the mother. Did he seriously just adopt a girl out of the blue? "Isn't it unusual for a single man to be allowed to adopt a young girl? I mean, no offence to you personally. It's just that it seems like . . . I mean . . ." I swallow hard as I try to say what I'm thinking without sounding prejudicial. But political correctness and gender-equality aside, if I'm an adoption agency rep there's no way I'd approve something like—

"It *is* unusual," Cain says, his eyes narrowing but not in anger. "And it wouldn't have been approved if I . . . if I weren't Maggie's biological father."

6

CAIN

She already knows more about me than all the women in my life put together. Which isn't saying much, considering there *are* no other women in my solitary life. Still, that's fucking meaningful, I think as I look down into her brown eyes, see that mix of emotions all over her pretty round face like she couldn't hide it if she tried. I can see that she's trying to decide whether to believe me or not, trying to figure out if I'm crazy or for real.

Then I hear a noise to our left, and my senses snap back into focus and I'm alert like an animal in the night, eyes wide as I remember why I'm here, what I came here to do, what needs to be done now.

Coco hears it too, and she turns in that direction and then glances up at me like she's wondering if perhaps I'm not nuts after all.

"It's just the pipes," she says, but I know she doesn't believe it.

"This building doesn't have radiators for heat."

"Well, maybe it's just the building settling," she says.

"Concrete and steel doesn't settle," I say, almost laughing when I see she's enjoying this in a perverse way, like she's decided that she's coming along for the ride, opening herself up to my story, perhaps making it *our* story. "Should we investigate?"

"Obviously," she says. "That's exactly what the idiots do in every dumb-ass horror movie. Hear a noise in the basement and head straight for it." She puts her hands on her hips—fuck, those hips—and looks up at me with a raised eyebrow and a cute-ass half-smile. "Lemme ask you this, Doctor Genius. Even if you're right and I'm wrong, what exactly do you expect to accomplish here? What exactly do you expect *me* to accomplish here?"

I look at Coco and frown. Suddenly I'm at a loss, and I rub my eyes until they burn. Fuck, maybe I *am* delusional. All the signs are right there in front of me, aren't they? Years of closing myself off from intimacy, from deep relationships. Obsessing over someone I believe killed my daughter years ago. Tracking this mysterious Doctor Death to some no-name hospital in some minor American city.

"And now I'm in an empty basement, hearing pipes clang and imagining it's the FBI cleaning their guns or whatever?" I mutter out loud. "Fuck, maybe I *am* a paranoid delusional. When you're in it you don't know that you're in it, right? That's why it's called a delusion. That's why it's called paranoia. Hell, maybe there *is* no Doctor Death. Or maybe *I'm* Doctor Death! Maybe I blamed myself for Maggie's death. After all, I was a doctor who couldn't save his own baby girl's life!" I look down at Coco as I talk out loud, babbling like I'm drunk or some shit. "What am I doing? What the fuck am I *doing*?!"

"You're doing what comes naturally," Coco says, and she's so calm I wonder if I'm hallucinating too. "Look, Cain. I believe that you lost your daughter in a tragic way. People deal with death in strange ways, all of which are natural in some sense. As for the rest of what you believe about how Maggie died . . . I don't know if that's real or not. In fact at first I was convinced it *wasn't* real. But the very fact that *you're* questioning it now is making me wonder . . ."

"Wait, are you suggesting that my delusions might be real? That my paranoia might be justified?" I say, not sure if she's messing with me or not.

Coco shrugs, her boobs moving beneath her scrubs in a mesmerizing way that reminds me that through all this craziness I'm still hard for her, like my body is totally focused on what it wants despite the way my brain is writhing and twisting itself into knots.

"Well," she says, glancing towards our left. "They *have* been doing this mysterious construction for over a year. This is a reasonably new building, so there really *shouldn't* be that much work needed. Besides, it's been really quiet for the past few months. Not even that many workers around. Maybe there *is* something going on, Cain." She looks back up at me, and I see the sharpness in her soft eyes, see something that makes me wonder how sweet and innocent this curvy creature really is. "Only one way to find out, isn't there?"

"I get it," I say, exhaling slowly and smiling at her. "You're just humoring me. Telling me what I want to hear. Look, Coco. I'm sorry. I'm not going to hurt you. You can . . . you can go. I need to figure this shit out on my own. Figure *myself* out. Maybe I need . . . need to get help."

"You've *got* help," she says firmly. "You've got me."

I almost break as I see the strength in her eyes, hear in her voice a sincerity that makes me think the outside world doesn't matter, that this is about what's in here and not out there.

And what *is* in here, I wonder, glancing around at the empty hallways and then back into Coco's eyes.

Just this.

Just the two of us.

Just the here and now.

"Why are you still here?" I whisper, my voice trembling as I see the answer in her eyes, feel it in my voice, hear it in my head. "Why are you trying to help me when I just threatened your life?"

"I told you earlier: Character is about effort. Compassion and kindness is hard work. Empathy takes time and patience. That's what love is, Cain. Taking the time to do the hard work of understanding someone, putting yourself in their shoes, seeing what they see, feeling what they feel."

"Sounds like a pain in the ass," I mutter, grinning and shaking my head at this surprising nurse, this woman who's standing her ground, standing beside me, shrugging and saying sure, let's go down this path you believe will lead you to whatever ending you're seeking. Let's see where it leads. Leads us both.

"It *is* a pain in the ass," she says. "I mean, look at the pain you've put yourself through for love, Cain. Love *is* a pain in the ass. But you can't avoid it. You can't escape it. You can't run from it. So the only option is to run *towards* it."

"Is that what I've been doing?" I say, not sure if I'm talking to myself or to Coco. "Running towards love even as I held on to this hate for so long? Hate for someone that might not even exist? Hate for someone that might be *me* for all I fucking know?!"

Coco shrugs and then nods. "That's why I won't leave, Cain. I won't leave you alone with your hate. Maybe you are Doctor Death, maybe all this shit is in your head, a twisted result of the guilt and help-lessness from losing your little girl. In fact, that's the most logical explanation. The research says that intelligent, educated men are least likely to seek help, so it's totally possible you created this Doctor-Death-and-the-FBI story without realizing it was just a crutch, a self-manufactured support to get you through a crisis." She shrugs again. "And you know what? That's OK. We all need a crutch sometimes. We all need support."

I stay silent, mesmerized, fucking *hypnotized*. This woman is wise beyond her years, smart beyond be-lief, exuding a strength that's shining from her eyes, flowing through her body, pouring out of her damned soul and right into mine.

"So now I'm offering you *my* support," she whis-pers. "Let *me* be your crutch. Which means you can let go of that other crutch and lean on me until you can walk again." She glances towards the empty hall-ways that are silent like a graveyard at night. "Go on. Kick open every door, bust into every closet, fake wall, secret hiding place. I'm here for you no matter what you find. Or don't find."

"What if I find that there is no Doctor Death," I say, blinking as a I feel both a chill and the most mag-nificent warmth flow through me at once, like I'm so close to breaking through a dark cloud that's en-veloped me for ten long years. "What if I discover that *I'm* Doctor Death?"

She widens her eyes and then winks. "Better than

discovering that this deserted hospital wing really *is* a secret government operation with men in black suits and aviator sunglasses."

"Sunglasses indoors? That's ridiculous," I say with a grin, feeling a giddy lightness whip through me with such force I almost pass out. Again I get that distinct sense that maybe this entire night is about us and nobody else, and in a flash I decide that you know what, there *is* nobody else! No secret feds doing something sketchy in a hospital basement. No clandestine "Doctor Death" running around cackling like a madman with a dripping syringe. Years in medical school and medical practice and I'm still constantly surprised by what the human mind and body is capable of doing, the way it twists and turns and contorts itself to fit some version of reality that's convenient.

Well, *this* is my reality now, I think as I turn all my attention to Coco, to this woman who turned my head around in the ER and is now turning my entire life right-side up just before it spiraled into a hole from which I might have never emerged.

"Maybe I did lose my grip on reality after what happened to Maggie," I whisper, the confession that I might actually be less than perfect, might actually be vulnerable, might actually be . . . *human* shaking me as I open my soul to this woman I've just met. "But I'm awake now, Coco. I feel awake, alive, reborn. This is my reality now, Coco. *You're* my reality now, and I'm not letting go of this version of my world."

And as I hear that silent clock ticking down to the New Year, I lean in, pull her close to me, and kiss her.

I kiss my reality into existence. I kiss away the past.
Kiss myself into the future.
  Into my forever.

7
COCO

His kiss enters me like a living, breathing thing, and I swoon against the wall as I feel myself lose my grip on the real world. The blue pastel walls swirl around me like they're alive, and one moment it's like I'm floating through a cloudless blue sky, the next moment I'm drowning in the deep blue sea.

But through it all comes that kiss, and it blows away all my thoughts and objections, all the protests and arguments, all the silly, mundane, real-world considerations that he's my boss or he needs help or maybe he's even dangerous, unhinged, violent.

Because that kiss tells me the truth:

He's mine.

I'm his.

And this story is about *us*.

"This night is about us, Coco," Cain whispers against my cheek as he pushes me up against the wall, his strong hand firmly gripping the back of my neck. He kisses me again, hard and deep, before breaking away once more and looking into my eyes. "I knew it when I saw you across that ER. There is no Doctor Death. It's a mind-trick, a lie I told myself for years just to make it through the day, to deal with my grief, my guilt, my anger."

"Well, it looks like we're dealing with something else now," I say, gasping as I feel his hardness press against my crotch, bringing forth my wetness to the point where my damp panties are now soaked. I'm almost dizzy from the strange mix of seriousness and playfulness, the odd way our minds are grappling with heavy, deep topics while our bodies are just shrugging and saying, "Whatever. Can we get on with it, please? Stop complicating matters with your big, mammalian brains. Less talk, more action."

"Shoulda dealt with this the moment I saw you leaning across the table," growls Cain, licking his lips and grinning as he glances down between us, where his tented scrubs are firmly jammed between the V of my thighs. I can see his thickness through the cloth, feel the massive head of his cock throbbing against my crotch. He's harder than the wall behind me, and I gasp again as he rubs my neck and then pulls my top down hard until my boobs pop out of my V-neck scrubs.

"Oops," I whisper, looking down at myself and seeing my secret black dress stretched to breaking-point as Cain kneads my heavy breasts and growls again like he's getting ready to pounce.

"Little black dress under your scrubs?" he mutters. "Well, well, well. Lemme see. Come on."

"Um, no," I say, color rushing to my face as I try to hold on to my loose scrubs. But Cain is too strong, and he pulls off my top, rips the drawstring off my

bottoms, and just straight-up *tears* the rest of my
hospital-issued uniform right down the middle of my
backside until I'm standing against the powder-blue
walls in a black dress that's still hiked up over my
hips. "Ohmygod, I'm *so* embarrassed!"

"You're so fucking sexy," Cain groans, grabbing my
wrists before I can pull my dress down and cover the
crotch of my beige panties. "What was I even thinking, waiting this damned long to make you mine."

"Um, it's been like an hour since we met," I say, even
though that totally doesn't make sense. It feels like
it's been a year, a decade, maybe forever. "Oh, shit,
Cain. What are you . . . oh, God. Oh, my *God!*"

I almost come in my panties as Doctor Cain drops
to his knees, slams my ass against the wall, and bur-
ies his face into my crotch with such force my slit
spreads like it's smiling. Before I know it he's pulled
my panties down past my ass and is gripping my buttocks firmly as he licks me with wild abandon, sucking
my stiff clit, running the flat of his tongue all along
my slit until I'm dripping down his chin and onto the
floor. Then he's inside me, his tongue sliding into my
cunt so deep it's like I'm being fucked.

"You taste like honey," he mumbles into my bush,
eating me like he really is a madman. "And you smell
like a flower. Fuck, I want you so bad. I want to con-
sume you, Coco. Swallow you whole. Make you mine
so completely I don't think I can hold myself back."

"Don't," I moan, leaning my head back as I feel that
embarrassment evaporate like mist in the morning
sun. "Don't hold back, Cain. Don't hold back."

I buck my hips into Doctor Cain's face, and he curls his tongue up against the front wall of my vagina, making me come all over his nose and face, my wetness gushing out like a river, in a way I didn't even think was possible. My vision goes blank as I jerk my head back and scream. But Cain keeps tongue-fucking me, and when I feel his finger slide confidently into my asshole from behind in the most shockingly filthy way, I come again so damned hard my knees buckle and I have to grab his thick hair to stop from falling.

I feel him rip my soaked panties off me, and then I'm on the floor, thighs spread wide, legs held up in the air by my ankles. Cain grinds his face all over my pussy again before leaning back and furiously undoing his scrubs, which are peaked and throbbing, a dark wet patch spreading as his cockhead oozes pre-cum in anticipation of entering me, claiming me, owning me.

"You're so warm," Cain mutters as he fingers me with one hand and pulls down his scrubs and underwear with the other. His cock bursts out like a spring, releasing from his underwear with such force it sprays pre-cum all over my mound and belly in the filthiest, most beautiful way. His big thumb taps on my clit like he's simply *commanding* me to come, and my eyes go wide as another climax rolls in like a goddamn freight train.

Then Cain is inside me, deep inside, his thick cock spreading my labia so wide it hurts in the most wonderful way, his cockhead driving so deep it feels like I'm being fucked for the first time, the only time, maybe the last time.

I'm thrashing and howling, dripping and squirting all over the hospital floor as the night's events pound into me like Doctor Cain's powerful hips. He's got me flat on my back, one hand cushioning my head from the floor, the other clawing at my sides, grabbing my ass, pinching my nipples as he fucks me so hard I'm literally *vibrating*.

Before I know it Cain is coming inside me, and my eyes flick wide open as he lets out a throaty roar and blasts a torrent of semen so far into me I almost choke. I wrap my legs around his muscular ass as he keeps pounding into me, yelling and shouting like a deranged mad doctor, his stethoscope still wrapped around his thick neck that's bulging and popping with veins. The vision of him holding me down and taking me is so raw and insane that I just scream with laughter, give myself to the madness, ignore all the warnings that my supposedly sensible brain has been trying to toss in there.

But it's too late for anything sensible, and with a guttural groan Cain rams himself into me one last time, his heavy balls slamming against my wet underside and clenching as he pours the last of his load into my womb and then collapses on top of me.

We pant together in the silent blue hallways of the hospital, and I take huge breaths of air, shuddering as my lungs fill with the aroma of our hot bodies, my wet sex, his thick semen. Cain is gently kissing my neck, his cock still hard, still deep inside me. My legs are still wrapped around him like I couldn't let go if I tried, and I giggle as I feel his seed slowly ooze out from my crease and make its way down my asscrack to the floor.

"That orgasm almost killed me," Cain groans. "I think I'm gonna start calling *you* Doctor Death."

I giggle again. "Well, I'd have to go to medical school before we can make that official."

Cain laughs and kisses me full on the lips. Then he props himself up on his elbows and looks down at me with those deep green eyes, sending a shudder through me as I realize that in just an hour we've opened up to each other, claimed each other, decided that this is our story, our night, our forever. It suddenly seems so simple. So easy. So perfect. God, what was all the fuss about in the first place?

"We *are* going to make it official," Cain says, holding that intense gaze. "Marry me, Coco. Tonight. In the hospital chapel. Marry me. I won't take no for an answer."

I blink and move my lips as I feel reality melt away until I'm not sure if this is a dream or an hallucination. Whatever it is, it can't be real. He can't really be asking me to . . . to . . . to *marry* him, can he? Who gets married after an hour together?!

Drunk folks in Vegas.

Teenagers in mad love.

And crazy people.

"Ohmygod, you really *are* crazy," I mutter as a smile breaks on my face. It's a smile I can't stop, and it's filling me with that overwhelming giddiness that's defined the mood of the day, made everything seem simple and clear even though a part of me knows it's complicated as hell, unclear and murky like a river dredging up mud, unearthing what's been buried, bringing what's hidden up to the surface. "Cain, we still have so much to learn about one another. Don't

you want to get to know me before asking me to . .
. to . . ."

"I don't recall *asking* you anything, Nurse Coco,"
Cain whispers down to me, a lopsided smile on his
brutally handsome face that's shining with a light
that I know is coming from me somehow. "Look, I
know how this sounds. But in medical school they
told us that although we like to think that what we're
doing is science, a doctor needs to remember that a
lot of it is art. We're still learning about the human
body. Hell, we know almost *nothing* about the brain,
about the secrets hidden in our DNA coding, about
the mindboggling complexity of hormones and en-
zymes, about why one person gets sick and another
is immune." He pauses and swallows, taking a slow
breath that I can feel in my own body like we're one.
"And we know absolutely fucking nothing about human love, Coco. Sure, we know about evolution and
the need to reproduce. But what makes us want one
person over the other? Yes, animals have pheromones
that signal when they're in heat. But scientists so
far haven't discovered any human pheromones. So
human attraction is still kind of a mystery." Cain
smiles and kisses me delicately, gently, like he . . . like
he *loves* me? "Except it's *not* a mystery at all in some
ways, is it? When you love someone it's clear as day.
It's crisp as night. It's vivid like a photograph. Just
because we haven't discovered precisely what chem-
icals get released when you fall in love, just because
we can't explain it in a scientific journal, put it in
a medical textbook, teach students in a classroom

about it doesn't mean it isn't real. Hell, Coco, maybe it's the *only* thing that's real!"

Cain rolls off me and pulls me into his hard, broad body. We lie together in the surreally empty hallway of the East Wing, and I frown at the blue walls, getting the strange feeling that they're just painted cardboard, just a mirage, a cosmic trick, that they're gonna just fall away to reveal giggling pixies and laughing elves, cherubs clapping their pudgy hands, cupids pointing their little arrows at my big bum as they take aim.

"You know how vision works, don't you?" Cain says as I snuggle into him and listen like I'm a girl hearing a bedtime story. "It actually takes a fraction of a second for the eye to transmit the signals to the brain, and another fraction of a second for the brain to put together the image that we call sight. But even a fraction of a second is actually a relatively long time, so what the brain does is serve up an image of what it *thinks* you're gonna see a fraction of a second in the future."

"What in heaven's name are you talking about, Cain?" I mumble as I listen to the mad doctor explain how the human eyeball works as we lie naked together on New Year's Eve. "Are you seriously saying that what we see is actually not what's happening right now but what the brain thinks is going to happen in the future?!"

"Exactly!" Cain says, glancing down at me like he's surprised I got it so quick. Sexist asshole, I think with a smile. "In fact we *never* see the world as it really is in the moment. We're *always* looking at a projection of the future. Isn't that fucking *wild*?!"

"Among other things," I say, running my hand along Cain's hard, chiseled body, tracing my fingers along his big pectorals, his tight nipples, his hard abdomen rippling with muscles so defined that I bet they could use it in medical school. Or art school.

"So in some sense it means that our bodies *know* the future, can anticipate what's coming. And maybe that means fate is real. Destiny is real. You *can* know you're meant to be with someone in just a moment, just a flash, maybe a minute, easily an hour! I knew you were mine the moment I saw you, Coco." Cain shrugs and raises an eyebrow. "The moment I saw your ass, actually."

I burst into surprised laughter, opening my mouth wide in mock indignation and smacking his bare chest. "OK, you really *are* an asshole!"

"That may be true. But what's wrong with that comment? It's true. I saw your ass and I knew you were mine."

I shake my head as I fight back laughter and embarrassment. "OK, look. Every woman is super-conscious about how big her ass is, all right? And when you've been a larger woman all your life, you're even more sensitive to comments like that."

"Oh, so you're *offended* that the sight of your big, beautiful bottom turned me the fuck on? Or are you just offended that I was honest about what I feel. What I want. What I damned well *need*."

Cain pulls me back down to the floor and cups my ass firmly, looking me in the eyes with a half-smile, his cock hardening again like it's backing up his argument.

"Oh, so now you need my *ass*? I don't even know what that means, let alone what it—"

And I can't speak anymore because Cain parts my rear cheeks and places his thumb firmly on my asshole, looking me dead in the eye as a wave of arousal flows through me.

"That's another thing that distinguishes us from most other animals," Cain whispers as he slowly kneads that big thumb into my dark rear pucker as a low moan escapes my lips. "Almost any part of our bodies can stimulate arousal with the right partner. Almost anything can be an erogenous zone. Do you agree, Nurse Coco? Do you feel it, Nurse Coco?" He draws close and licks my lips as I feel my rear hole relax and open up in the sickest, dirtiest, most lovely way. "Do you want it, Nurse Coco?" he growls, prying my asshole open with two fingers and sliding a third just past my forbidden opening. "Will you take it, Nurse Coco? Open wide and say aaah for Doctor Cain?"

I want to laugh but the arousal is making me choke and chortle, and I lick my lips and just nod. Immediately Cain sits up and flips me over, and I groan as he grabs my hips and raises my ass. He spreads my asscheeks wide and holds them spread. I know he's looking shamelessly at my most secret space, and I let him do it as I feel myself opening up in every possible way to this man, to this moment, to this crazy night before New Year's.

"Aaah," I say, opening my mouth wide as Cain starts

to lick my asshole and rub my slit from below. He fingers my cunt and then reaches up along my naked body, pinching my breasts and putting his fingers into my mouth even as he drives his tongue into my anus. I suck his fingers and hunch my body over, the feeling of being owned, possessed, dominated roaring through me as I come violently just from being penetrated orally and anally, like the Doctor is proving that he doesn't even need to touch my clit to make me climax!

"We'll need some lubrication, Nurse Coco," he whispers from between my buttocks, and before I know it he's moved around me and is on his knees directly in front of me.

I gasp when I see his massive cock sticking straight out like a log, thick and heavy, curving upwards, its head huge and glistening. I blink in surprise, and then I nod and lower my head, opening wide as Cain grabs my hair and slowly pushes his throbbing cock past my trembling lips.

"Oh, fuck," he gurgles. "So warm and soft. I need to go deeper inside. Open your throat. Ah, that's it, Nurse Coco. Ah. Aah. Aaaaah."

I almost choke on his cock as I realize now it's the Doctor saying "aah" even as I open wide for him. It's been a long time since I did this, but clearly my body knows exactly what to do for my man, and I feel my throat open up for Cain's thick shaft like we were designed for each other.

Soon he's balls deep into me, all the way against my face, carefully fucking me in the mouth as I sit up and suck him until his pre-cum and my saliva drips down the sides of my mouth. But I keep going, harder and harder, reaching below him and grasping his heavy balls, making him roar in pleasure.

Cain's got two hands on my head, fingers entwined in my hair and gripping tight. I'm totally under his control. But he's also under my control, I realize as I massage his balls and roll my lips and tongue over his cock. The realization sends another wave of arousal through me—arousal that makes me seize up and come again even though I'm not touching my clit or fingering myself. The sensation is sublime, and I blink away tears as I feel something click inside me, something wild and wonderful, something that can't be described in words but feels clear as day, crisp as night, vivid as a photograph . . .

"I love you, Coco," Cain mutters as he pulls my hair, rubs the back of my neck, tightens his ass and hips, and then just *explodes* down my throat. "Oh, fuck, I love you."

I just nod as my eyes go wide and I gag and choke at how he's emptying his balls yet again into me, pouring his thick semen down my throat this time like he wants to take me in every hole, claim me in every crevasse, own my every orifice.

I'm overflowing down the sides of my mouth, and just when I think I can't swallow any more and Cain can't possibly *have* any more for me to swallow, he pulls out of my mouth and turns me away from him roughly.

I scream and spit as I feel him pull my ass up and smack me hard on the bottom, twice on each cheek. "The best for last," he growls, spanking me again until I scream in submission, spread in shock, stick my ass up as I feel the sting of the Doctor's dominance.

A second later he spits on my asshole, spanks me nice and hard once more, and then rams his thick, throbbing cock all the way into my ass.

All the way.

Every inch.

Every damned inch.

8

<u>CAIN</u>

Somehow I'm still coming as I feel Coco's magnificent ass open up for me. I can barely see straight, and my balls are still clenching from how hard this curvy nurse made me come with her lips and tongue. But fuck, I *am* still coming, and I just shake my head and mutter like a lunatic as I see her rear hole gape wide for my thick shaft.

Soon I'm all the way into her, shocked and thrilled that she can take all of me into all of her. But this isn't just me taking what I want. This is also me *giving* what I want. There's no denying the obvious design of the human man and woman, the simple truth that I yearn to penetrate her just like she yearns to take me into her.

"But you've entered me too," I whisper as I start to move inside her distended asshole, my semen and her saliva smoothing the entry as I glide back and forth in her clean canal. "You're under my skin, Coco. In my head. In my heart. Part of me now. Mine, just like I am yours. That's the miracle of human love, of how a man and woman bond for life, how they enter one another in ways that are more than physical."

I feel Coco come as I push back into her, massage

her shoulders as I hold her down, pull her thick brown hair as I empty more of me into her even as I feel her enter me in a more subtle, deeper way that's spiritual, magical, more real than the flesh, more eternal than the air.

I shoot the last of my load into her, groaning and digging my claws into her buttocks as I seize up and release. I feel my lips move, but I can't say a damned thing.

Because I'm fucking spent, done, vanquished, broken.

Healed.

I collapse on top of her and just start laughing as I remember why I came here, think of the insane journey of solitude and madness that was ten years in the making. That shit I said about how the brain and eye work together to make it look like we're seeing the now but are actually seeing an image of the future is real science. But the idea that we somehow get drawn to the person we're going to bond with even if the first meeting is *ten years* in the future . . . yeah, that's stepping outside the realm of science.

And into the realm of love.

Into the realm of forever.

9
COCO

You came for what felt like forever," I say as Cain lovingly wipes my ass and thighs with his shirt and then dabs his own cock, which is still oozing his seed. Seed that he poured into every hole I have. "Is that cause for concern, Doctor Cain?"

"Are you saying I have big balls, Nurse Coco?" he says, his voice muffled because his face is buried in my mussed hair.

"I don't know what I'm saying," I murmur, closing my eyes as I fight back reality. "I don't know what I'm thinking. I don't know what I'm doing." I swallow and look up at him, thinking of what he asked me earlier. Or what he *told* me earlier. "I don't know what *we're* doing, Cain."

"It's called pair-bonding," Cain says in a comically clinical voice. Then he smiles and kisses my forehead. "Which civilization now calls marriage. *That's* what we're doing, Nurse Coco." He raises an eyebrow as he strokes my side. "You can keep your last name if you want. Hyphenated, of course."

"Are you gonna hyphenate *your* last name, Doctor Asshole?" I say as I shiver under his warm touch, melt in his hot gaze, feel that pesky reality retreat to the sidelines like it knows it's not gonna win, that this night has spiraled out of orbit and it's not even midnight.

Cain sighs and glances at his Rolex—which is the only thing he's wearing. "Nah. I don't want to get new business cards. Besides, Doctor Cain-Asshole works fine for me."

"I thought it was Doctor Death," I tease, quickly closing my eyes and wincing. Shit, I just gave the real world an opening, and now I'm thinking about it, aren't I. Thinking about how little I know about this man.

How much do I *want* to know, I wonder as I study the lines on his face, glance at the streaks of silver in his dark hair, the gray in his stubble. He's handsome as hell, but clearly he's also *been* through hell. If I say yes to this, am I saying yes to heaven or hell?

Again I think of his name. Cain. Nobody names their son Cain, do they?

Don't be ridiculous, I tell myself. I bet lots of sweet, wonderful boys are named Cain every year by reasonable, loving parents. Stop being paranoid, Coco. Also, stop having conversations with yourself.

"Did you name your daughter Maggie or did she . . . well, did she . . ." I say, realizing I can't hold back the real world anymore, that I need to ask the questions that . . . well, that need to be asked.

"Did she come with the name, you mean?" Cain says, still caressing my side like he's not surprised that I'm finally asking about his mysterious life, the twists that brought us together. "Yes. She was nine when I got her back, remember?"

"Got her back . . ." I say, blinking as I remember him explaining why he was able to adopt a nine-year-old girl as a single dude. "Oh right, you said you were Maggie's biological father." An image of a young, reckless, broke medical student jerking off in a jar every Saturday for cash comes to mind, and I snort and widen my eyes. "Ohmygod, don't tell me there are a hundred of your kids running around the world right now!"

Cain frowns and then laughs out loud, shaking his head. "Oh shit, no, Coco! It wasn't through a sperm bank or something. It was . . ." He swallows and exhales hard, glancing at me and then looking away for a moment. "Someone asked me, all right?" Now Cain's face has lost that light, and I see his green eyes darken again. "It was a patient of mine. A sweet, compassionate middle-aged woman who'd lost her husband before they had a chance to conceive. She was in her late forties, and she'd decided that it just wasn't her fate to be a mother." He snorts and shakes his head. "I was a young, headstrong, hot-shot doctor, with full faith in the power of science to overcome any limitation of the human body. I told her she shouldn't give up, that artificial insemination worked wonders these days, that she was healthy enough to carry a child, that she *should* chase her dream of being a mother if that's what she felt inside."

I just stare at Cain, not sure what to think, what to feel, maybe even what to believe. "So she asked *you* for . . . for *sperm*?"

Cain grits his teeth and closes his eyes. "I was seeing her pro-bono through a volunteer organization where I donated my time and expertise. Her deadbeat husband had left her in debt, their finances in shambles. I told her I'd handle the procedure for free. I'd even pay the sperm bank fee. But she didn't want to pick some guy out of a book or whatever. She wanted it to be someone she knew. She asked me if I'd . . . if I'd donate." He shakes his head and forces a smile, but I can see that he's terrified. Terrified that I'm going to get up and walk away. "Listen, Coco. I'd just convinced this woman not to give up hope. And so how could I say no after I gave her hope like that?"

Slowly I roll away from Cain and sit up against the wall. I pull my knees up against my chest and hug my legs, rocking back and forth as I try to come to terms with what this man just told me.

"Coco, look at me," Cain says, his eyes wide with desperation like he's worried he's lost me. "Hey, there was nothing between us, OK? The topic of sex never even came up. It was always just about—"

"You think *that's* the biggest issue here?" I snap, blinking about a hundred times in the span of a second. "It would almost have been less shocking if you'd just fucked a patient ten years ago and gotten her pregnant. But something like this . . . God, Cain. I . . . I don't know how I feel about that decision. I really don't. I mean, clearly it's an ethical violation—or multiple ethical violations. You'd lose your license if anyone found out." Then I frown and cock my head. "Wait, but people *did* find out, didn't they? You said this woman died and you got custody of Maggie because you proved you were the biological father. So how are you still a practicing doctor if the authorities found out you'd donated your own sperm to your patient and performed an unauthorized procedure to get her pregnant?!"

Cain looks at me like a twelve-year-old who's just been caught stealing his dad's car. He shrugs sheepishly and then just grins and holds his big, muscular arms out. "Um, well, I lied. I just told the family court judge we had sex after she was no longer my patient. The DNA tests confirmed Maggie was my daughter. Case closed."

I almost collapse in a mix of disbelief and straight-up laughter at how this story has descended so far into the comically insane that there's nothing to do *but* laugh. And so I just laugh, laugh like a freak, like a madwoman, a lunatic on a full-moon night.

I laugh like a woman in love.

"I love you," I manage to say through tears of pure emotion. I still don't know if what he did was sickening or heartwarming, but I know that I fucking love him. The truth is, what he did is both sickening *and* heartwarming. It would be one thing if Cain had used his position of authority and expertise to force her to accept him as a sperm-donor out of pure ego or narcissism. I remember hearing a story about a gynecologist who secretly swapped out his own sperm when he was performing artificial insemination for his patients. That guy got off on the thought that he was spreading his seed far and wide. But Cain? No. For all the ego and confidence oozing from this man who just took me as his woman, that's not part of his

DNA. He might be crazy, but he's not a megalomania-cal psycho. He might be a rule-breaker, but somehow his heart is still in the right place.

But what about his head, I think as I reach out for the arm he's holding out to me. Is that in the right place? After all, an hour ago he was talking FBI-conspiracies, witness protection, and doctors who kill children for fun or some shit! Is it really possible that it was all a delusion that his traumatized brain came up with to handle the loss of a child he'd made a conscious—perhaps questionable—decision to help bring into this world? And if so, is it possible that the two of us coming together, "pair-bonding" as he calls it, suddenly "cured" him of the decade-long delusion?! Fuck the crazy out of each other?! Seriously?! Does that shit even happen in romance novels anymore?!

"Maybe in that insta-love trash all the nurses read in the break room, their faces going flush as they shift in their chairs and feverishly flip through their phones and eReaders," I mutter as I rub my aching head and look at this bad-ass, maverick doctor staring down at me like he's not sure if *I've* lost *it* or if *he's* lost *me*!

But I know he hasn't lost me. In fact he's *won* me. After all, what I just did with him is an ethical violation too, isn't it? We just broke so many rules even the Boards of Health, Medicine, and freakin' Labor Statistics or whatever wouldn't be able to count! I'm a rule-breaker too, but my heart's in the right place. Kinda. Sorta.

"Right here," I whisper, looking down at Cain's big meaty paw and prying open his fingers. I place my palm in his and look down. "Right here, Cain. That's where my heart is. You've got me. I'm yours, Cain. It might take me years to fully come to terms with the decision you made, but my heart tells me you did it for the right reasons and that you followed through like a man does, you stepped up and claimed your little girl when she needed her father. Yeah, you committed perjury by lying. But by stepping forward you were risking your career and a whole lot more. Maggie *was* your biological child, and in the end you did the right thing, even though it was most certainly on the edge."

I'm still shaking my head as Cain pulls me close and wraps me in his arms. I know we've got a long road ahead of us, that there's years of hard therapy ahead of Cain so he can unravel whatever made him believe the paranoid nonsense he did.

"But I'm here now," I whisper. "I'll be with you no matter what gets thrown at us, no matter what we have to deal with. This is us, Cain. This is us. Just the two of us."

Cain looks at his watch once more, and then raises an eyebrow. "Three," he says.

"What?" I say.

"Two," he says with a grin, turning his watch towards me so I can see that it's almost midnight. "One!"

I squeal and gasp at the same time, and one second later Doctor Cain kisses me hard on the lips and growls in a fake Elvis-Supervillain voice that seems to confirm this was all a dream, a dream of the future, a dream that's called my life:

"Happy New Year, baby," he says. "Happy New Year."

And as I kiss him back and almost hear the fireworks pop around us, almost feel the tinsel and streamers fall down on us, almost hear the cheers and applause from the invisible audience of mythical creatures watching from behind the blue cardboard walls, almost feel my happily-ever-after get rung in with the New Year, I get the strange feeling that something's not quite right, that maybe instead of a New Year's Fairy Tale this is the part of the Cinderella story where reality comes bouncing in like a pair of pumpkins.

Pumpkins in black suits and sunglasses, that is.

"Sunglasses indoors?" I mutter as I stare at the two men in black suits and mirrored Aviators who've busted into the hallway and are pointing their weapons at us. "Now that's ridiculous."

10

CAIN

"That's ridiculous," Coco is saying as I pull at my bonds and strain my neck to look at my woman. "There's no way this is real. There's no way this is happening. There's no way the East Wing of my little hospital is really some secret FBI medical facility! Absolutely not. Wake up, Coco. Wake the hell *up*!"

"Wait," I say, frowning and blinking as I turn to my curvy nurse who's cuffed to the chair beside me. "So you were more comfortable believing that I was fucking insane, a paranoid delusional? You should be *relieved*, Coco!"

"Relieved? *Relieved*?!" she screams. "We're handcuffed in an abandoned hospital just past the stroke of midnight! When did this turn into a horror story?! This was supposed to be a love story!"

"The hospital isn't abandoned," I say with a calmness that only seems to drive Coco deeper into her rage. "It's just the East Wing. Just take it easy, honey. I'll get us out of this."

"I'm waiting, Doctor Asshole," she snarls, blinking and shaking her head as she strains at her cuffs.

"Are they fighting?" says Baldhead-Sunglasses to Squarejaw-Sunglasses.

Squarejaw grunts and rubs that big square jaw with his gun like he isn't worried about blowing his own head off. "Huh," he says. "Let's watch *this* for awhile. To hell with that weird-ass sit-com you think is funny."

"You just don't understand the ironic genius of self-referential absurdist humor," complains Baldhead, sighing and rubbing his clean-shaved head as I start to wonder if I'm in a fucking cartoon.

"What I don't understand is any of the words you just used," quips Squarejaw, grinning like he's pleased with his little joke.

"Like *that's* a surprise," snaps Baldhead. "I thought the Bureau didn't hire high-school dropouts. Which higher-up is your dad?"

"Hey, this is *our* fucking story," I shout at the two squabbling FBI-goons. I'm smiling like a deranged man, and Coco is still talking up a storm, like she needs to keep talking just to keep herself from losing her shit. "Don't bring your drama into it."

Baldhead smiles and holds his hands up. "Oops. Sorry, Doc. Go on. We'll be quiet. This is way more fun than watching some kidney-thief breathe through a ventilator and piss into a bag."

"Kidney-thief?" both Coco and I say at almost the same time.

I frown as I'm suddenly taken back to the night my Maggie died. She'd been diagnosed with something I apparently missed when I tested her myself, in my own clinic. After getting a second opinion from a well-respected doctor—the man I eventually came to blame for Maggie's death—it turned out she had a defective . . . kidney.

A kidney that the man I called Doctor Death insisted needed to be removed.

A procedure that cost little Maggie her life after she got an internal infection that couldn't be controlled, that spread through her little body, stopped her tiny heart, broke my goddamn soul.

I'd tried to destroy Doctor Death's career, get him for malpractice or something. But he was repeatedly cleared by the Board, and when I finally decided to take matters into my own hands, finish him myself, the goddamn Feds popped up and took him away for something.

I used every contact I had, pulled every string I could, but no one could tell me where they were holding Doctor Death or even why the Feds had picked him up. It was only when I heard a rumor that the Feds were doing black-ops stuff like the CIA, using civilian facilities and unmarked places to hold people for longer than they were legally allowed, that I started keeping my eyes and ears open, asking my contacts in the government more specific questions.

And then, a few months ago, an old patient of mine with contacts in the Bureau told me that just before he retired he'd used his last favor to get his contact to run Doctor Death's name through the database.

And he got a hit.

A no-name hospital in a no-name town.

This hospital.

This town.

This night.

This woman.

I glance over at Coco, and our eyes lock as if this night just got so fucking weird that not even Bald-head's favorite genius-absurdist could get away with putting it in a story. Certainly not a love story.

But this isn't just any love story, I think as I signal with my eyes that I love her, that this is still *our* damned story, that this needed to happen before the night could become morning, before the darkness could be dispelled, before we can ride off into the sunrise or sunset or whatever the fuck people do when they get to the happy ending.

"Nah, it's not just any old love story," I say out loud, not sure who I'm talking to. "It's *our* love story. And it's gonna get sewed up tight tonight. Every loose end tied up. Every dangling thread neatly snipped off." Then I look squarely at Squarejaw and boldly at Bald-head. "All right, talk. You're both federal agents, and you're not going to put two in our heads and bury us in the woods. So you might as well talk. The asshole you've got pissing in a bag killed my daughter. I could never prove it, but I always knew it. That diagnosis was phony. No way I missed something that he found. But all right. I'm not a specialist, and I had to defer to the more qualified expert. I would've spent a year getting a hundred different opinions, but Maggie's condition was dire. She needed action, not more fuck-ing research. So I let go of my pride and ego for the sake of my daughter. I trusted science, put my faith in what the reports and scans and the more-qualified expert was telling me. But now I know I was right. He did it. No way it's just a coincidence that you called him a kidney-thief when his diagnosis showed that Maggie needed her kidney removed. A young, healthy kidney that could be sold on the black market."

Squarejaw rubs his jaw and Baldhead rubs his head. I can see that the sincerity in my eyes and the authority in my voice is getting through to them. Still, they're FBI, and even if this night has turned into a surreal cartoon, I can't expect them to simply shrug and tell us everything about a case that's off the books even at the Bureau.

"But wait," I mutter as excitement lights me up like a pop-rocket. "If you're holding Doctor Death here in secret, off the record, then it doesn't fucking matter if you tell us everything or not, does it? I mean, if you're worried that we'll do an expose in the *Times*, the FBI have total deniability. In fact, no reputable news agency will print a story without multiple independent credible sources."

Squarejaw looks over at Baldhead and grunts. "You understand all that jargon?"

Baldhead raises a well-plucked eyebrow and sighs. "You know what? You're right, Doc." Then he shrugs. "Doesn't matter anyway. Your Doctor Death isn't coming out of his coma. That's why they put him in this off-the-books location in the middle of nowhere. We've been watching him for six months, waiting to see if he'll wake up and give us the testimony we want so we can take down this ring."

"Ring? What do you mean?" Coco says sharply.

I glance at her ring-finger and grin. I almost wink at her, almost whisper to her to hold her horses, that the ring will be forthcoming immediately following the dramatic conclusion.

"Kidney-smuggling ring," says Baldhead, his face grim as he adjusts his sunglasses. "You know that thousands of Americans die every year waiting for kidneys. And a lot of these folks on the wait-list are rich enough and desperate enough to buy a kidney on the black market."

"Hundreds of doctors involved," says Squarejaw proudly, like he did all the investigating himself. "In every American state. Places you'd never expect. Doctors you'd never expect."

Baldhead sighs again. "We offered Doctor Death immunity if he gave us a full list of all the other doctors involved. But he refused. He said they weren't criminals, that the organ-donor system was broken, that healthy people didn't need two kidneys, that we needed to share the wealth."

"Yes, but *voluntarily* share the wealth!" I roar, pulling at my cuffs as I think about Doctor Death making a choice for my little Maggie—a choice that wasn't his to make. Wasn't *anyone's* to make! It was her choice and hers alone. Her body and hers alone. "There's nothing more personal, more intimate, more your *own* than your fucking body. The man's not just a murderer. He's a monster. The real crime is that he's still alive! That you fuckers offered to let him walk!"

"He was never gonna walk," growls Squarejaw softly, and my eyes widen as Baldhead glances over at him like maybe his dimwit partner is spilling too many damned beans, exposing too much of the FBI's dirty laundry. "That's why he's here. With us." He glances at his watch and taps it even though it's digital. "Hey, it's past midnight! Time's up! We get to pull the plug and close this fucking dead-end of a case!"

"Pull the plug? You mean . . ." says Coco.

"Yes," says Baldhead. "They told us to give it until the end of the year. The year just technically ended, and Doctor Death is still pretty much brain-dead. It's over." He nods at me. "You've got the ending you want, Doc. We gotta wait until the lead on the case gets here with the clean-up team, but the moment we're done you guys are obviously free to go. You're right. Even if you tell everyone, you'll just be grouped with the rest of the conspiracy-theorists."

"Don't ask, don't tell, right?" says Squarejaw.

Baldhead groans and rubs his head, shaking his fist like he can't even deal.

"No," says Coco suddenly. "We have to give it more time. We can't let him die. Not if there are hundreds of doctors out there literally *stealing* kidneys by manufacturing fake ailments and running a black market in organs right beneath our noses."

"You got experience waking someone up from a coma?" says Baldhead drolly.

"Why yes, I do," Coco says softly.

"You do?" I say to her, smiling even though I want Doctor Death dead and gone. "Who?"

And Coco just looks at me calmly and smiles. "Me," she says softy. "Me, Cain."

11

COCO

"I have the same genetic defect that killed my brother. It wasn't fatal for me, but when I was a kid I was in a coma for almost a week. I actually remember it. I remember coming out of it. My parents brought me back. They . . . they just read to me. That's all they did. Didn't matter what they read, they told me later. Storybooks, magazines, journals, whatever. It was about the sounds of their voices, their persistence and focus, the fact that they just wanted me back, that they refused to let me go," I say to Cain as I hold his hand and feel the anger roil his hard body. "And it worked. They pulled me back into this world from wherever I was. I followed the sound of their voices like it was a trail of breadcrumbs. I followed it all the way back home. Back to them." I pause. "Back to you, Cain. To us." I squeeze his hand tighter, knowing that he wants this man dead but is holding back because he knows there's something bigger at stake, more lives at stake, lives of people we've never met and might never meet but that still matter as much as the lives of those we know and love.

"This is what compassion is, isn't it?" Cain finally

says as he slowly sits beside me near the comatose body of Doctor Death. "This is what you were trying to tell me earlier, that while sometimes love comes spontaneously and easily, like it did with us, sometimes it takes effort, intention, time and patience. It takes character. Moral character that's beyond rules and regulations, that answers to a higher calling, responds to the greater good."

"I said all that?" I say softly, glancing down as I feel the admiration in his gaze, the love in his touch, the bond between us getting stronger even as we turn together towards a man that deserves no love, no compassion, no forgiveness. "Well, you picked a wise woman to marry, Doctor Asshole."

"Would an asshole be opening page one of a fucking kid's book and reading to the man he's fantasized about killing for ten years?" Cain mutters. "Wait, this isn't a children's book. What the hell kind of book is this?"

"It doesn't matter, honey," I whisper as we hold hands and start reading together, like we're Mommy and Daddy in the strangest fairy-tale ever written. "Because in the end there's only one story, Cain. You got your name from the Old Testament, didn't you? And that started with the greatest story ever told. The story of the fall from grace and the endless effort to find our way back to the Garden of Eden, back to oneness and union. It's the story of man and woman, Cain. The story of us, repeated through the eons, twisted and contorted but still the same, eternal and unchanging, always and forever."

The story of love.

This year and the next year.
The first year and the last year.
Now and forever.

∞

EPILOGUE
NINE MONTHS LATER
COCO

I look down at my newborn daughter Cassie and then up into her father's green eyes. The labor was short and smooth, the delivery calm and peaceful, like a dream, a fairy-tale, pure perfection.

"She's perfect," Cain whispers, pulling down his hospital mask and slobbering all over Mommy and Baby without giving a rat's ass about protocols and silly nonsense like germs. No germs in this fairy-tale.

"Did you think about what I asked you?" I say after giving Cain a moment to soak in the pure beauty of our baby girl, witness the miracle of new life, the joy of new beginnings.

But even new beginnings can tie in to old stories, and I see the emotion on Cain's handsome face as I think about what I'd asked him when we found out I was having a girl.

"You want her middle name to be Margaret," he says quietly, his voice trembling. "Are you sure, Coco?"

"Are you OK with that?" I say, not sure if I'm honoring his lost child or introducing a painful reminder into every day of Cain's life. "I mean, there are a hundred other names that are beautiful too. But I just thought . . . I mean, it was your Maggie who in some way brought us together, put you on a collision course with me. But if it's too painful, then—"

"It *is* painful. But it's also beautiful," Cain finally says. I know he's thought about it deep and hard, and so have I. At some level I didn't want to burden our little girl with heavy memories of someone else. But I have faith that neither of us are going to see it that way. In some ways it establishes continuity, like one year moving into the next year. A new year that's its own year but still connected to the past. Middle name seemed like a good middle ground.

"Margaret," Cain says out loud. "I like the sound of it. It sounds smart and dignified. Margaret it is. Cassie Margaret."

We cuddle together after the hospital staff congratulate us and leave the room. Then I see Cain's expression change again, and I know that he's heard something . . .

Something about Doctor Death.

I think back to that strange New Year's Eve, when we'd sat there and read to a killer in a coma, read for hours and hours, on and on with faith and perseverance, both Cain and I reaching deep inside ourselves and pulling out the best of what we had, finding the source of what drove us to become healers, helpers, men and women who swore first and foremost to do no harm.

It seemed hopeless at first, but then Baldhead had muttered something about a blip on the brain-scan readout.

Then the blip became a beep.

Finally a buzz.

Of course, Doctor Death didn't suddenly sit up in bed and start talking. But the scans showed enough brain activity that the FBI decided to keep him on life support a bit longer.

Long enough, it seems . . .

"He regained consciousness for two hours apparently," Cain says. "Gave up the location of an encrypted hard-drive in a locker somewhere. It's got all the doctors, victims, and even the recipients of every kidney stolen and sold. A massive coup."

"Ohmygod, that's incredible!" I say, smiling and then seeing that Cain is strangely melancholy. "Oh wait, that means . . . oh, God, Cain, it means you must also know who actually got Maggie's kidney. Did you ask them?"

He nods slowly. "A little girl who was on dialysis with two failing kidneys. Maggie's kidney saved her life. That girl is still alive. Still healthy. Still smiling." He blinks and I can see the conflicting emotions clear as day in his green eyes. It was still wrong and unjust and unforgiveable, but at least someone else lived because Maggie died.

"What else?" I say, knowing this isn't the time to talk about what Cain just found out about where Maggie's kidney ended up, that at some level this is his burden, his conflict, his weight. When he wants to share it with me, I'll be there. But I can see there's something else in what the FBI told Cain, and a chill goes through me when I see what looks like guilt flash across his face.

"Two hours," Cain says. "He regained consciousness for two hours and then went back into a coma." Cain swallows. "And the Feds gave the order to pull the plug. They in effect executed him. Decided he wasn't worth taxpayer money any longer."

I gasp, instinctively shielding Cassie's little ears. I'm horrified at the cold calculation, the ruthless administration of what I know is justice. But that's part of the story, isn't it? Part of the drama. Part of the madness. Part of the ending.

"It's over, Cain," I whisper up to him. "Over and done."

"Nah," says Cain, grinning that cocky asshole's grin as he pulls his new family close and we all smile like it's a postcard. "It's just the beginning. The beginning of something new. Something happy. Something forever."

Always new.

Forever new.

Happy New Year, baby . . . ;)

∞

FROM THE AUTHOR

All my love for the New Year ahead.

New year, new series!

THE CURVY FOR KEEPS SERIES (USA)
Bargain for the Boss
Given to the Groom

Not through the holiday books yet?

Taken on Thanksgiving
Captive for Christmas
Night Before New Years

And here's my full-length novel series: CURVES
FOR SHEIKHS and CURVES FOR SHIFTERS!

And if you wish, do join my private list to get five
never-been-published forbidden epilogues from
my SHEIKHSseries.

Love,
Anna.
mail@annabellewinters.com

PS: For my international readers:
Annabelle in UK
Annabelle in CA
Annabelle in AU
∞

Books by Annabelle Winters

The CURVES FOR SHEIKHS Series

Curves for the Sheikh
Flames for the Sheikh
Hostage for the Sheikh
Single for the Sheikh
Stockings for the Sheikh
Untouched for the Sheikh
Surrogate for the Sheikh
Stars for the Sheikh
Shelter for the Sheikh
Shared for the Sheikh
Assassin for the Sheikh
Privilege for the Sheikh
Ransomed for the Sheikh
Uncorked for the Sheikh
Haunted for the Sheikh
Grateful for the Sheikh
Mistletoe for the Sheikh
Fake for the Sheikh

The CURVES FOR SHIFTERS Series

Curves for the Dragon
Born for the Bear
Witch for the Wolf
Tamed for the Lion
Taken for the Tiger

The CURVY FOR HIM Series

The Teacher and the Trainer
The Librarian and the Cop
The Lawyer and the Cowboy
The Princess and the Pirate

The CEO and the Soldier
The Astronaut and the Alien
The Botanist and the Biker
The Psychic and the Senator

THE CURVY FOR THE HOLIDAYS SERIES
Taken on Thanksgiving
Captive for Christmas
Night Before New Year's

THE CURVY FOR KEEPS SERIES
Bargain for the Boss
Given to the Groom

WWW.ANNABELLEWINTERS.COM

∞

Made in United States
North Haven, CT
23 June 2023

38132828R00054